D1095798

39204000007936

FAERIEGROUND

The Fate of the Willow Queen

Book Eight

BY BETH BRACKEN AND KAY FRASER
ILLUSTRATED BY ODESSA SAWYER

STONE ARCH BOOKS
a capstone imprint

FAERIEGROUND IS PUBLISHED BY
STONE ARCH BOOKS
A CAPSTONE IMPRINT
1710 ROE CREST DRIVE
NORTH MANKATO, MINNESOTA 56003
WWW.CAPSTONEPUB.COM

LIBRARY OF CONGRESS CATALOGING-IN-
PUBLICATION DATA IS AVAILABLE ON THE
LIBRARY OF CONGRESS WEBSITE.

ISBN: 978-1-4342-4492-5 (LIBRARY BINDING)
SUMMARY: AT THE CROW PALACE, SOLI TRIES
TO SAVE HER FRIEND. BUT DOES SHE HAVE
THE STRENGTH?

BOOK DESIGN BY K. FRASER
ALL PHOTOS © SHUTTERSTOCK WITH THESE
EXCEPTIONS: AUTHOR PORTRAIT © K FRASER
AND ILLUSTRATOR PORTRAIT © ODESSA
SAWYER

PRINTED IN THE UNITED STATES OF AMERICA
IN STEVENS POINT, WISCONSIN.
032013
007227WZF13

"Hope is the thing with feathers—"
Emily Dickinson

For my parents, Tom and Susan Bracken, who taught me how to build a nest. —b
Dedicado a mi abuela Luisa Zorrilla, el angel que me enseño a volar. —k

Not all wishes are good wishes.

And in Willow Forest,
the faerieground still waits,
just past a wish in the
woods . . .

Chapter 1

Soli

Jonn, Kheelan, and I run toward the Crows' nest, holding hands.

Lucy waits in the Crow palace, somewhere.

She's dying.

This is the fastest I've ever run.

The Sirens are nearby, and I know I'm not to

listen to them.

I've heard of Sirens. We read about them in

school. I never knew they could be real. They

have a song, the legend goes, that takes you in.

I think I'm strong enough to hear it and not

give in. What could a song do, anyway?

Then I hear the whispers. I hear them calling
my name.

Their sweet song.

Come to us, Soledad.

Come to us, princess.

Wouldn't it be so much safer, so much better,
to be there with them? To give up my crown,
to give it all up.

Come to us, Soledad.

Come to us, princess.

And I stop running.

I let their song swim into my heart.

Chapter 2

Lucy

I wait in Caro's room.

I know I should be mad at her—I am mad at her, in a way—but mostly I feel bad for her. She thought that stealing me away from the Ladybirds would get her some attention. And I don't think it's going to work. She's not going to get what she wants.

The door opens, and Caro walks in, carrying a tray. She puts it on the bed in front of me. "Don't spill on my bed," she tells me, turning up her nose.

I pull the tray closer. "I won't," I say.

There is a bowl of some kind of thin soup.
A hard roll. A glass of brackish water. Prison
food.

"You're still dying, you know," she says. Like
she's telling me the weather.

"I know," I say. "I didn't think the milk, or
whatever it was, would cure me." It gave me
my sight back. That was all. My body still feels
hot and sick.

"Bee pollen, I think," she says. "And probably
some other stuff."

"Yeah, I assume," I mutter. I wish she'd leave, but she sits down at the other end of the bed.

"I know you want me to leave," she says. "But this is my room."

"I know," I say. I sip the soup. It needs salt, but it's warm. "I didn't ask to be put here. You brought me here."

"Sorry about that," she says, and I look up at her. She does look sorry. Then she sighs. "It's not that I don't like you, Lucy," she says. "I just needed to do the right thing for my father."

"I get it," I say.

"He doesn't want to lose the Willow Kingdom. It's important to him. He wants to win the war. And we were so close—until you and Soli came here. We were almost done. The queen would have died and we would have taken over and it would be ours."

"But then the queen's daughter came back," I say, suddenly understanding. "So now they'll try to use me to get her to leave. They'll say they'll only cure me if she leaves. Right?"

Caro stands up, her face flushed. The soup sloshes out of the bowl and onto the tray. "Shut up!" she says. "I never told you that!"

Chapter 3

Soli

I sway with the music, toward the music, toward the whispers.

Toward the Sirens.

I close my eyes.

But then hands grasp my shoulders.

I open my eyes. Kheelan's face blocks my sight of the Sirens, his hands over his ears. I push hard against him, trying to see them again. He covers my ears, and I can't hear the voices anymore. My self floods back.

But now Kheelan can hear the Sirens.

"Cover my ears," he yells, and Jonn comes toward us. I reach up and cover Kheelan's ears. Jonn has his own hands clamped against his head.

"Run," Jonn mouths, and his eyes dart toward the black castle beyond the lake.

At the same moment, Kheelan and I take our hands from each other's heads and put them on our own, and in the brief second my ears are open, the sweet voices slide in again.

But I keep my eyes on Kheelan's.

I cover my ears. I turn my body. And we all run, again, toward the nest where the Crows live.

When we are far enough away from the lake, Jonn lowers his arms. Kheelan and I do the same.

"That was awful," I say. "I didn't think it would be that hard."

"You did a wonderful job," Jonn says. He smiles at me.

"Thanks," I say. "But it was Kheelan's help that got me past." Kheelan grabs my hand, and I squeeze his fingers.

The forest is open here, in the valley where we stand at the foot of a rocky hill. The Crows' castle seems so far in the distance.

"There's a shortcut," Jonn says. "Calandra said to follow the sound of the water."

My eyes swell with tears, but I don't let any of them fall.

As we walk, I am the first to hear it. "I think I hear a waterfall," I say.

Jonn tilts his head to the side, and he nods. "I hear it too," he says. "Come."

The sound of water becomes overwhelming as we climb to the top of a large boulder. There's a waterfall beyond it, falling from jagged, dark rocks.

"There," Jonn says. He points. "We cross that water."

Chapter 4

Lucy

Caro storms out of the room, but I know what I said was right.

I will die unless Soli agrees to leave. But if she leaves, her kingdom falls to the Crows.

I finish every bite of my food. Whatever happens, I'll need as much strength as I can get.

Then I gaze out the window for a while. I try to imagine what it would be like to be Caro. For this to be my life.

The grounds outside the castle are beautiful, even if there are guards tromping back and forth. And her room is warm and pretty.

Her father is someone important, so she's had privilege and luxury. I imagine her bossing around servants. Wearing beautiful dresses. Having fancy parties. Being Caro, not Caro the Betrayer.

I stand and begin to look around the room.

A chest of drawers holds her clothes, but I don't want to invade her privacy by going through them. I slide the drawers closed without touching the silk and leather and woolen clothes inside.

A shelf is lined with books and little trinkets—

shells, pinecones, dried flowers. It reminds

me of the things my mother would leave at the

edge of the woods for the faeries. The things

she did to keep Soli—and me—safe.

An armoire made of dark wood stands in the

corner. I tug at the doors, and though they are

hard to open, one side finally does.

The wardrobe is full of weapons. Girl-sized

ones.

So this has been Caro's life.

Chapter 5

Soli

The water is fast. The water is cold.
The water is everywhere.

I've rolled up my jeans, but my clothes are soaking.

We walk in a line, not touching each other. First Jonn. Then me. Then Kheelan.

If one of them falls, we have agreed that we have to let him fall. If I fall, they will save me.

I argued, but they would not listen.

They work for the queen. And now the queen is me.

I can't look up. I can't look anywhere except into the water, to watch where I place each foot.

A rock is slick with weeds, and my foot slips, but Kheelan, swift as a fox, reaches forward. He holds me steady until I have my balance back.

I still don't dare to look up, to look anywhere besides down at my feet on the rocks in the water.

My heart pounds.

And when Jonn reaches for my waist and pulls me onto shore, I am shocked.

"We made it," I say. He nods, unsmiling. Then he helps Kheelan to shore.

The Crows' castle-nest looms ahead of us. "How do we get in?" I ask. "What's our plan?"

Kheelan and his father look at each other. "We are just your guides," Jonn says finally.

I feel panic rise in my throat. "So . . . we don't have a plan?" I ask. "What am I supposed to do?"

"No one can tell you that," Kheelan says. "You are the queen."

"There is one thing," Jonn says. "I can help you one way."

He pulls a vial from his pocket. "Your mother used this often," he says. "It's liquid magic. She had none of her own, so——she needed its aid. It will help you."

Something makes me stop, pull my crown from my backpack, and place it on my head.

He holds the little glass vial toward me. Inside,

a dark liquid swirls.

"I don't need it," I tell him. "I have magic of my

own."

Chapter 6

Lucy

On the bottom of the wardrobe full of weapons lies a boy's cap.

A leather coat is crumpled at its side. And a pair of boots sits in the corner of Caro's room.

Suddenly I know what to do.

I put on the cap and shove my hair under its brim. The coat is too big, but the sleeves aren't so long that I look like I'm wearing my dad's coat. The boots fit perfectly. I toss my shoes under the bed and try the door.

It opens. I don't know how much longer I'll be able to see, so I have to go now.

The hallway is empty, but once I turn a corner guards are everywhere. I keep my head lowered, and no one stops me. They all act like I'm not even there.

I don't know what it is, but something is telling me to keep walking. And the same something tells me to stop at a plain wooden door, and to open it.

It's a storage closet, or something. Just shelves and buckets and brooms. But when I look up, I see a wooden box on the top shelf.

I climb up and grab the box. Inside, there's a necklace a lot like the one my mom used to wear. The one with the pendant that's now in Soli's crown.

But this pendant is blue, not green.

I wind the chain around my throat and clasp it.

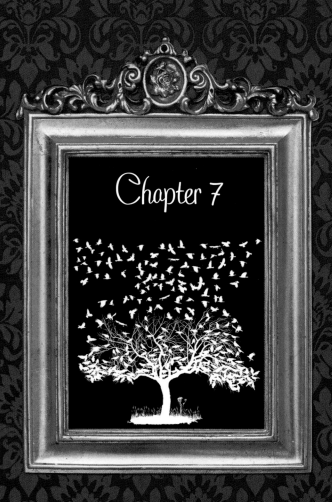

Chapter 7

Soli

My magic has stopped the guards.

It has opened the door. It has let us into the nest.

All I have to do is touch the stone in my crown, and what I want is what happens.

The Crow guards shout, but we don't stop. We walk slowly down the hallway, and they have to let us pass by. They raise their weapons, but they can't use them. The magic won't allow it.

It's as though Lucy is calling my name: I know where to go.

We walk faster, faster.

Once we find Lucy, I will get the Crows to heal her. I don't know how, but I will. I know it in my bones. And then we will go back to my kingdom, where I will help the people heal.

One more room. Then a hallway. And then we'll find her. I don't know how I know, but I do.

We march through a set of wooden doors into a room. And my magic suddenly can't help anymore.

Caro stands in the room. And beside her, a man. He wears a crown.

"Queen Soledad," he says.

He bows, but his nostrils flare as if Jonn and Kheelan and I are disgusting to him.

"I'm here for my friend," I say.

"She is safe, and still alive," he tells me. "Do you dare to doubt me?"

"It doesn't matter whether I doubt you," I say.

I can feel that Lucy is alive. I don't know how I know, but I do.

"You sound like your mother," he says, walking closer. "And look like her, too."

The man reaches for my chin. I see Caro wince.

"Don't touch her, Georg," Jonn says.

"Protecting her, are you, Jonn?" the man— Georg—says. "Just like the last queen, I suppose."

"That is my job," Jonn says, straightening his back. "I am sworn to protect the Willow Queen."

"And who is this?" Georg asks, gesturing at Kheelan.

"He is my son," says Jonn. "And my apprentice."

"Sworn to protect the queen," Caro says, a mean smile spreading across her face. "I knew there was a reason he was paying attention to you."

"Be quiet, child," Georg says, and Caro's smile disappears.

I try to call forth the magic, to quiet Georg so that I can find Lucy. She's just down the hallway. I can feel her there.

"Your magic won't work in my presence," he says.

"That's what you think," I mutter. I reach up and touch Andria's pendant, safe in my crown.

The king, if that's what he is, is enjoying this.

He moves his hand and my own hand goes
numb, falls to my side.

"Just like your mother," he says again. "And like
her, you'll never reach what you came for. And
like her, you will have to choose."

He points at Kheelan. "The boy, or your
friend," he says. "One of them must die. You
choose Lucy, I'll kill the boy. You choose the
boy, I'll let the girl's sickness kill her."

And just like that, my eyes fill with tears.
"Both," I whisper.

Chapter 8

Soli

"Choose Lucy," Kheelan says. "It's okay, Soli. I promise."

"No," I say. "I won't choose against you. And I won't choose against her."

"Both was never an option," Georg says.

He moves his hand again, and a shoot of pain courses through my body.

Suddenly I understand my mother, my real mother.

She had to choose. It was a different choice, and it ended up trapping her.

I won't make the same mistake.

"I have made my choice," I say, and my voice

sounds clear and strong.

Chapter 8

Lucy

I know Soli is here. I don't know where, but I can feel her in this castle somewhere.

I leave the closet, the necklace I found around

my neck, the pendant clasped in my hand.

There's noise in a room down the hall. I think I

hear Soli's voice, and Caro's, and her father's.

And just as I reach for the doorknob, I look up.

I'm no longer standing inside the Crow palace.

My vision is clear and my fever is gone.

I'm in Mearston, at my own house, and the

door has opened and my mother stands there.

Chapter 9

Soli

I had to choose.

"Both was never an option," Georg told me, and as soon as he did I knew he was wrong.

I could save both of them. So I chose.

"I have made my choice," I told him.

Kheelan grabbed my hand. "You must choose to save Lucy," he said. "I have promised to die to protect you."

I held on to his strong fingers, and then I let his hand go. I could not look at him.

I knew Lucy was nearby. I felt more connected to her than ever. Something was pulling us together, like magnets.

My head felt clear. I felt strong.

"We are waiting, your majesty," Georg said with a sneer.

"I need a moment with the queen," said Jonn.

He pulled me aside. "You don't have to choose," Jonn whispered. "We can fight Georg, and we might beat him."

"He's strong," I whispered back. "We can't beat him."

"We can send for help," he said.

"What did my mother do?" I asked. "Didn't he make her choose?"

Jonn sighed.

"He made her choose which sister would be sent home," he told me. "Andria, who was becoming a Crow, or Calandra, who wanted to save Andria."

"And she chose to save Andria," I said.

Jonn nodded. "She chose to stay."

"Why isn't he asking me to make the same choice?" I asked, but as soon as I asked it, I knew.

Georg expected me to choose to save Lucy. He thought I would choose Lucy, and Kheelan would die. And then to save Lucy, I would promise to leave. And then my kingdom would be left for the Crows to take.

"We are waiting," Georg said again.

I could still feel Lucy's presence in the castle. She was alive. She would be safe.

I straightened my back. I looked at Georg.

"Have I changed your mind?" Jonn whispered.

"No," I said. "I've still made my choice."

"I cannot protect you if you've chosen against our kingdom," Jonn said.

"I choose myself," I told Georg.

He frowned. "What do you mean?" he asked.

I could tell that I'd surprised him. Things weren't going according to his plan.

"I choose myself," I said again. "Like my mother did."

Then I reached up and touched the stone in my crown, and in one wish, I wished Kheelan home to the kingdom, and I wished Jonn home to the kingdom, and I wished Lucy home to her mother.

And now I am here with the Crows, all alone.

Chapter 9

Lucy

My mother is glad to see me.

I tell her everything that's happened since we left. It's only been a few days, but so much has happened.

My sickness. The trip to the Ladybirds. How Caro took me. And then how I was in the Crows' palace, and how suddenly, I was home.

"I'm so glad you're safe," she says. "I don't understand, though. How did you get home?"

I shrug. "I don't know," I admit. The pendant still hangs around my neck. I pull it out. "I think it might have something to do with this."

She gasps when she sees it. "Where did you find that?" she asks.

"In the Crows' palace," I say.

She is quiet, looking at the necklace. "Mom, I know about you," I say. "How you went to the faerieground and everything."

"You don't know everything," she says. "Some things only I know."

And she stares out the window and into the forest.

Chapter 10

Soli

Because I am a queen, they don't put me
in the prison cells.

They won't sink so low. They have manners.

"Unlike your people, who tossed me—a princess—into a prison cell," Caro says, bringing me my supper. "We treat royalty with kindness here."

"In a locked room?" I mutter.

She tosses her hair. "Kindness. Not freedom," she says.

That's a fair point. I understand.

"But it wasn't me who locked you in that cell,"
I say.

She rolls her eyes. "I know that," she says. "But
it was your people. That's how things are here.
You have so much to learn."

It seems like I'll have lots of time to learn, too.

I sent Kheelan and Jonn away, knowing they
will take care of my kingdom. I sent Lucy
home, knowing that she'll be safe. And she
won't be able to come back, not without me.

So I am all alone with the Crows.

Caro slams out of the room. The wooden door shakes, and I hear a key turn in the lock.

They think I'll try to escape. There's a guard outside my door.

But I won't.

I have the feeling there's something here I need to learn. Something I have to do. A missing piece of an important puzzle.

The food Caro brought isn't prison food. A thick slice of meat. A bowl of salad and a cup of soup. A hunk of bread and a plate of cheese. A little cake topped with berries.

It occurs to me that the food might be poisoned, but I think they know they can't kill me. If they kill me, someone else in my kingdom will become the leader. But while I'm here, I'm the queen, and the kingdom is leaderless.

Except for Jonn, who will do the right thing.

I want to stay strong while I'm here, so I eat. Every bite.

Then I lie back on my bed and stare at the wall. The walls in this room are made of polished gray stones, so dark they're almost black.

There's not much else in the room, besides the bed—a chair, a little chest of drawers. I get up and open the drawers. Inside are some clothes. A nightgown, a soft pair of pants, a few cotton dresses, even some underwear.

Everything seems to be for a girl who's older
and taller than me.

Underneath the underwear there's a gray
T-shirt. Printed on the front are the words
"Mearston Meteors."

That's the team name at the high school in the
town where Lucy and I live.

And then I realize these must have been my
mother's things.

She must have stayed in this room.

Shocked by this new knowledge. I go back to the bed and sit down.

Then I stare at the stones that make up the wall.

I remember the last thing she said to me. "Remember to always turn the stones."

I stand again, walk to the wall. I move my hands over the stones. One sticks out farther than the others, and I try to turn it, but it doesn't move. I keep trying, touching all of the stones.

Finally, one shifts when I touch it, and I am able to wrench my fingers around it and turn it until it comes loose.

Behind the stone, there's a little hole. And in the hole is a folded piece of a paper.

I pick up the paper. Underneath it is a key, which I slip into my pocket.

When I unfold the paper, dried four-leaf clovers fall to the floor. I scoop them up and put them in my pocket, too.

I write this to the next girl who sleeps in this bed, who waits within these walls. I know I won't be the last person to come to this room. Whether I do what they ask or not, they'll take another prisoner. They'll pretend to treat her kindly. They'll feed her delicious food and fatten her up and let her lose her fear. Then they'll tell her what she has to do.

Oh, I have so many questions and no time for answers. How can I kill someone? How can I pretend to love someone and then kill him? How could Andria want to be here, want to be with these people? How could she be in love with that awful man? He doesn't love her.

Do not trust the Crows. Do not believe them when they tell you they'll keep you safe. Do not care about them. Don't even try. Not even if someone you love begs you to try. The key unlocks your door. Someone I trust gave it to me. But before you turn it, you must be ready to go. I didn't have time to make a plan. I have to come up with something, something that will work. Or I have to kill the man they want me to kill.

Good luck to you. That's what the clovers are for. Maybe you'll have magic on your side. I'm just a girl. I don't have much hope.

Calandra